Coffee Talk 3

Coffee Talk 3

An Uncle and His Nephew
Discuss the Reality of Suffering

By

J.R. Dickens

This story is a work of fiction, but it sure has a lot of truth in it. Any resemblance between the author and the character named "Uncle Bob" is probably coincidental—although it's true the author's middle name is *Robert* and he has been an uncle since the age of eight.

ISBN (Print Edition): 978-0-9992870-2-6

Other books in this series:

- Volume 1: An Uncle and His Nephew Discuss the Nature of Truth
- Volume 2: An Uncle and His Nephew Discuss Faith and Science

Introduction

This is the third installment in the *Coffee Talk* series. The first book addressed the nature of reality and the logical absurdities of relativism. The second book took up the relationship between faith and science to show that modern science relies on its own religious (metaphysical) commitment. In this volume, we will undertake a difficult topic that eventually touches us all.

You'll see right away that this conversation has a noticeably more somber tone than the first two: we're confronting the reality of suffering and its tragic effects. There is no sugar-coating it. When our sense of fairness is confronted in such a personal way, we can't divorce ourselves from the intense feelings that come with it, so rather than try to dodge those feelings, we'll take them head-on. In the end, we'll see how our feelings must ultimately be guided by *truth*—and the truth about suffering cannot be understood by merely observing it happen. We must seek God's wisdom in a matter like this, and it will be Uncle Bob's task in this conversation to steer his nephew into the truth so that he can begin to see the purpose of suffering from God's vantage point. We mustn't follow the world's ideas in regard to suffering—namely, that it is *real*, but that it serves no good purpose. Instead, we must turn to the One who is able to bring good out of the worst examples of human suffering. Any reliance we place in our own strength is ultimately a false hope.

To help you navigate some of the more difficult terminology, several words highlighted in **boldface** are defined in the Glossary. You will also find a number of review questions in the back of the book that are suitable for individual or group study.

My hope is that this book with strengthen your faith in the one true God who is able to bring good out of the worst human suffering, and that you will be encouraged to seek him diligently.

J.R. Dickens

Woodland Park, Colorado

Chapter 1

It's been a rough week. If your troubles at work weren't enough to rattle your sensibilities, the news about your neighbor Michelle would still have thrown you into an emotional tailspin. And that's not all, because along with the tragic news of her diagnosis, you suddenly seem to be noticing more and more of the anguish that intrudes into people's lives every day. Some of it is certainly self-inflicted, but much of it seems capricious and undeserved. Anyone who says that 'life isn't fair' is making an understatement that deserves to be ridiculed. Why is your next-door neighbor facing a death sentence in the prime of her life? *If there is a God, where is he at a time like this?*

A stout pot of coffee is brewing as you anticipate the arrival of your Uncle Bob on a dreary Saturday morning. The two of you have spent a great deal of time together since you moved to town, and he's been able to help you understand some difficult concepts of philosophy, ethics, and theology. You're hoping he'll be able to help you unravel the hopelessly tangled knot of thoughts and feelings that have been plaguing you since you learned about Michelle's illness a few days ago.

A knock on the front door signals the arrival of your uncle.

Chapter 2

Your slightly soggy uncle steps over the threshold, folding a flimsy umbrella and defiantly stamping his shoes on the mat. “What a morning,” he intones without preamble.

“Thanks for coming over today.”

Removing his raincoat, Uncle continues. “The dreary weather seems to be a fitting backdrop for what may be a difficult conversation.”

“I guess you could say it feels like a dark cloud has been following me around all week.”

“I was very sorry to hear the news about your neighbor, and it’s understandable that you’re upset about it.”

“I was just getting to know her when I heard what happened.”

“Tell me more.”

Uncle follows you into the kitchen where the coffee is waiting. After filling your cups, the two of you take a seat at the kitchen table. In the silence of the moment, the only sounds are the patter of raindrops on the window panes and the rhythmic tick of the kitchen clock.

"About a week ago there was an ambulance in front of Michelle's house. I learned that she'd collapsed in the back yard. The doctors ran a bunch of tests and a found a tumor in her brain." You have to pause to collect your emotions. "They're telling her it may be operable, but the prognosis is still poor." Pausing again, you continue. "Either way, it doesn't look like she has long to live."

Uncle hesitates before speaking in a subdued tone. "What about her family?"

"She has a husband and two small kids. Ed runs an architectural firm. The kids are two and five years old. Eleanor and Justin."

The heaviness of the moment sinks in as raindrops continue to tap gently against the windows. A long, low rumble of distant thunder rattles the panes.

Uncle takes a sip of coffee and stares into the cup before speaking again. "At a time like this, every fiber of your being is crying out for an answer to the question: '*Why?* Why does something like this have to happen?' And 'Where is God in all of it?'"

You can only muster a silent nod in reply. You're staring into your cup as well. Uncle may have to do most of the talking today.

Chapter 3

"The tragedy of suffering is often the reason why we begin to doubt the goodness of God. It's understandable. Especially when it's someone close to us—and especially when tragedy strikes someone who, by all outward appearances, is undeserving of it. Our minds struggle to make sense of it. We want answers. Desperately."

You collect your emotions—a strange combination of anger and sadness—just enough to respond. "Those little kids are going to grow up without a mom. Explain to me how that's fair."

Uncle is glad to see that you're able to give a voice to the thoughts and feelings swirling inside you, but for the moment he sidesteps your demand. He knows it wasn't directed at him. "When we're faced with a tragedy like this, it's natural to look for someone to blame. And it's quite tempting for us to place the blame on God."

"You say that God is good. You say that he controls everything." Stated as an accusation.

"And it therefore follows that *if* God is real, and *if* he's good, and *if* he's omnipotent, *then* he would never allow suffering and tragedy. It's the argument that many have used to justify their skepticism. Or their atheism."

"I suppose you could say it's 'justifying my skepticism' at this very moment." There's a tone of sarcasm and simmering anger in your voice.

"There's nothing wrong with the moral indignation we feel when faced with the reality of suffering. But we have to be careful that we don't direct that anger toward someone who doesn't deserve it."

"And I suppose you're going to tell me that

I shouldn't be angry at God right now?"

"You might be surprised for me to say that suffering breaks God's heart, as well."

After a short pause to let the remark sink in, you answer, "I think you have a lot of explaining to do today."

Chapter 4

Uncle has to tread carefully in looking for a reply. He wants you to explore your feelings but he doesn't want you to be led down the path of cynicism. "I will do my best to answer your questions. But I'm going to need your help."

"What do you mean?"

"We're dealing with some of the hardest questions anyone can ask about the character of God and about the nature of the human experience. It's going to take some patience on your part as we try to unpack it. We can't expect to answer every question all at once. We may not be able to answer them all in a single day."

"Okay." You can see that Uncle is trying to help you manage your own expectations.

He's also helping to defuse the building pressure for you to get the answers now.

"You know that I like to take a very methodical approach. If we want to answer these kinds of questions adequately, we should start with the big picture. But you'll have to trust that we're working back around to the place we started from."

Uncle is understating the case when he describes his approach as *methodical.* In your past conversations, it has often taken considerable effort to see how the pieces all fit together. But in time, it starts to make sense. Uncle tries to teach in a way that helps you ask the right questions in order to lead you to the answers. It's challenging, but effective.

Uncle continues to set the stage. "The struggle we face when dealing with the question of suffering is that, humanly speaking, we only ever see part of the whole. We easily see the 'temporal' part—the stuff that happens in the here-and-now, like Michelle's diagnosis, and the immediate effect it will have on her family. But there is a spiritual reality as well, and it turns out to be the most important part. We never know *all* of the spiritual reality, but part of it is revealed to us in the Bible."

You find yourself a bit uncomfortable with the spiritual angle, but frankly, that's where the big question lies. "So you're saying that if we want to understand why God allows suffering, we won't find the answer from human experience alone."

Uncle is encouraged by your reply. "We will not. And that is a big part of what the Bible does—it reveals who God is, and the nature of his character. It also helps us understand why he does what he does."

"But what about your statement a little

while ago—'If God is good, and if he is omnipotent, then he wouldn't allow suffering'? That seems airtight."

"The logic is good as far as it goes, but there's something missing from our **syllogism** if a good God who's omnipotent can allow suffering. There must be some additional **premises** that will lead us to a different conclusion."

"And that's why we need the Bible to help us get the answers?"

"Yes. But let me add that we are still left with questions. And the short explanation is that God doesn't tell us *why* he does everything he does."

Uncle's comment sounds like he's already making excuses for not providing all the answers you're looking for. "And why not?"

"The answer to that question is simple. It's because *he's* God and we're *not*. We have to remember that he doesn't owe us an explanation for *anything.* God answers to no one. When he *does* provides an explanation, our posture should be humble gratitude."

"You sound like you're talking out of both sides of your mouth. Does the Bible answer our questions or not?"

"Yes and no. And by that, I mean that the Bible answers the *general* question about why there's suffering and how God brings good out of it. But if you want an answer as to why Michelle *in particular* is suffering from this *particular* diagnosis, the Bible doesn't answer those kinds of questions."

"And I suppose you're going to tell me that we have to have faith at that point."

"Yes. Faith means trusting in the goodness of God and his purposes, even when we don't know all the reasons for what he does."

Chapter 5

The coffee break comes at a good point in the conversation. Questions are still swirling in your mind, but Uncle seems to know where the conversation needs to go. In fact, you suspect he's had to deal with these questions himself.

You put your notion to the test. "I have a feeling that this topic is personal for you." Maybe Uncle will take the hint.

He hesitates before responding in a vague way. "Anyone who's been around for a while has seen the reality of suffering and has experienced it firsthand. It raises the same kinds of questions in all of us."

You cast a look at Uncle that encourages him to say more.

He remains unusually evasive and abrupt. "Suffering is a universal experience."

In an effort to get Uncle to open up, you ask, "What was it that first brought you to the question of suffering?"

Uncle dodges the question again. "Let's just say that the tragedy of suffering hits us the hardest when we see it happen to those who are most vulnerable."

You're not sure what he means, but at that moment you're reminded that Michelle's diagnosis will have a ripple effect on her family. Their lives will certainly never be the same.

Uncle redirects the conversation. "Let's get one possibility out of the way. *There is no god.* In that case, whatever we may call 'suffering' is little more than the violent struggle for survival in a universe without purpose. There can be no purpose for suffering in a godless universe. In fact, suffering can't even be described in terms of good and bad."

You're now thinking back to your previous conversations with Uncle, and making the connections to the present discussion. "In other words, without God there can be neither **ethics** nor **teleology**. Or as you like to put it, 'stuff just happens.'"

"And if that's the case, we can stop here because there are no answers to our questions."

"You're trying to say that atheism is a dead-end philosophy."

"Indeed. No creator, no purpose, no morality. Now, another possibility is that there is a god, but he's either not good or not omnipotent."

You follow the lead. "If there's a god but he's not omnipotent, then he isn't really god."

"Right. He would have no power to change anything. And if that were the case, we could hardly blame him for not doing something."

"And if he were omnipotent, but not

good?"

"Once again we'd be unable to blame god for the reality of suffering. If he weren't good, he wouldn't have any reason to care. He might even be the cruel kind of god that some atheists see when they look at the God of the Bible."

"So the only way we could try to lay the blame at God's feet is if he were already both good *and* omnipotent."

"That seems to be the case. Which brings us back to the idea that we must be missing some information—something that makes it possible to preserve God's power and his character in light of the reality of suffering."

"And that brings us back to the Bible."

Chapter 6

Uncle diverges momentarily. "Remember when we talked about the difference between a **contradiction** and a **paradox**? Can you tell me which of those describes our situation?"

Uncle's question is helping you focus your mind, but it's not enough to know where he's leading.

He sees your brow furrow slightly and picks up his own thought. "It seems as though both sides are dealing with a paradox, but with the intent of resolving it in different ways. Let's give the other side some credit—at least they're attempting to use logic to resolve the problem."

At that moment Uncle seems to be having a conversation with himself, working out his thoughts as you gaze at him across the table.

"The critic will say that the explanation

for suffering is that either God isn't real or he isn't good or he isn't omnipotent—one or more of the premises is false. The paradox is resolved by changing at least one of the premises. The Christian would say that the paradox is resolved by filling in the *missing* premises that preserve God's power and his character while explaining how suffering still remains."

"So the critic gets it half-right?"

"The critic can't see how to resolve his own paradox in a way that preserves the integrity of God. Frankly, he doesn't want that kind of an answer, because his atheistic bias is to impugn God in a way that knocks him off his throne."

"So the critic doesn't really want to know the answer. The truth."

"We've discussed this problem before. The atheist objects to the existence of God on *moral* grounds, not *intellectual* grounds. God gets in the way of how he wants to live his life, so he wants to get God out of the picture—whatever it takes."

The earlier conversation is still reasonably fresh in your mind. To keep the discussion on track, you interject a question. "So, what's missing from the argument? How do we explain suffering without blaming God?"

"If God is both all-good and all-powerful—and suffering is real—then God must have a good *reason* for allowing it."

The rain seems to be picking up again.

Chapter 7

After a short break to stretch your legs, a fresh pot of coffee is now brewing in the kitchen as the two of you return to the conversation. The morning is almost gone and it won't be long before you're both thinking about lunch.

"If we want to understand suffering, we have to consider the beginning and the end," Uncle says in a paradoxical way. "The end means *death*, because we all die. The beginning means the beginning of creation—before death entered into the world."

"Science tells us that death is just a natural part of life." You make the statement somewhat self-consciously, in light of the previous conversation you had with Uncle about the philosophy of science.

"I want you to notice that you're taking us

back to an atheistic **worldview**. Death is the mechanism for evolution. Survival of the fittest. The weak die out, or they are destroyed by the strong. Suffering and death are features of the system. Not a nice world to live in."

That's not really where you meant to go, and Uncle knows it, but it's hard to resist the temptation to revert to popular explanations of reality.

"Maybe what I *meant* to say is that we take death for granted."

"In that regard, you're probably quite right. But why should we take death for granted and not the suffering that eventually leads to death?"

Uncle has a point. Now that you think about it, it seems like a case of selective reasoning to make such a big deal out of suffering but to then treat death as something natural—or even good. You offer, "I suppose it's inconsistent to see them as separate experiences."

"Maybe even contradictory, if we fall into the trap of treating death as an end to suffering, rather than an end *result* of it."

"And that's because some people argue that we should put suffering people out of their misery—like we would do in the case of animals?"

"Euthanasia—usually in the form of doctor-assisted suicide—is growing in popularity and has been legalized in several countries around the world, as well as several states here in the U.S. And where it isn't yet legal, it still goes on 'under the radar'—and probably has for a long time."

"But legalizing it doesn't make it *right*—just legal."

Uncle is pleased to see you made such an important distinction. "Again, we're faced with the question of ultimate moral standards. The Bible makes a distinction between killing animals and killing people. Popular culture is more inclined to see them as the same thing."

"And that's because culture—with **Darwinism** as its religion—sees animals and people the same way."

"Yes, quite observant. In contrast, the Bible makes a clear distinction between mankind and the rest of creation. And that means that the 'rules' that determine how we can treat animals are different from the rules for how we treat people."

"But what's the difference? Aren't all living things nearly the same at the cellular level—DNA, and so forth?"

Uncle leans back in his chair. "Biology doesn't define the difference between man and animal. The difference is spiritual."

"And if it's spiritual, then it's outside the

realm of something science can observe. What did you call it last time?"

"***Metaphysical***. Which now takes us back to the beginning of creation. When God created man, he gave man an immortal soul, and along with that soul, God gave man some of his own attributes. The Bible calls it the 'image of God.' The Latin expression is ***imago Dei***."

"So man is like God in ways the animals are *not*?"

"Correct. Man is the only being in creation that combines both body and soul. Animals have bodies without souls, whereas angels are spirit beings without physical bodies."

"But you said God gives man some of his attributes. What does that refer to?"

"Man is able to reflect some of the attributes of his Creator such as intelligence, creativity, and morality. Man's spiritual nature also means that he is able to relate to his

Creator, who is spirit."

"Do you mean that man's soul is designed to seek God? To connect man with God?"

"Yes, and man in turn is able to relate to his physical environs because he is also a physical creature—literally, a 'man of dust.' Man is able to 'exercise dominion' over the creation, as the Bible puts it. And that exercise of *authority* also reflects something of God's nature."

You are starting to see more of the connections. "We need the Bible to reveal these kinds of spiritual realities. There is no other way to discover them."

Uncle summarizes. "Science draws the wrong conclusions about the nature of man because science cannot observe what makes man unique."

"But we still haven't answered the questions about human suffering."

Uncle defers. “We’ll start to tackle that after lunch. This morning has been a good start. Now what’s on the menu today?”

Chapter 8

You decided to go "all-out" for lunch this time by picking up a deli tray with an assortment of cheeses and cold cuts. Uncle seems to be impressed as he begins to assemble a sandwich heavy on the meat and cheese. The variety of chips appears to be equally appealing as Uncle grabs a handful from several different bags before sitting down at the table.

Your mood has stabilized considerably since the discussion began this morning. The hard questions remain, but your cynicism is dampened even though your heart remains heavy as you think about Michelle and her family. There is a hard road ahead for all of them. The children will struggle to understand that mommy is sick and won't be with them much longer. Ed will have to make huge lifestyle adjustments even as he's grieving the loss of his wife. He still has a business to run—employees and clients who are depending on him.

Uncle senses your sinking emotions and tries to engage in some small talk to lighten the mood. "I understand you're soon getting some new responsibilities at work."

The change in subject catches you off guard. "Well, yes. My supervisor is assigning me to lead a new project team. It's not a big project, and the rest of the team has a great deal more experience than I do."

"It sounds like a test of your leadership skills." Uncle is devouring his sandwich as if time were of the essence.

"And that's what makes me nervous about it. I feel like I'll be under a microscope."

"*And you might fail miserably,*" Uncle adds, "*thereby proving that your supervisor's confidence was desperately misplaced.*"

Uncle's comment sounds utterly tactless except that it precisely expressed your own unspoken insecurities. "Um, yeah, so I'm feeling some pressure."

"I will only offer one small tidbit of advice," Uncle says as he chases sandwich with chips and washes it all down with a canned soda. "Just relax and have fun."

Uncle is really telling you that he knows you can do it.

Chapter 9

By the time lunch is finished, the rain has almost stopped but the thick gray clouds continue to threaten ominously. Rumbles of distant thunder roll through periodically, but it's hard to tell whether stormier weather is approaching or receding. In any case, it seems unlikely that you'll be spending any part of the afternoon on the patio. You and Uncle settle into the living room chairs.

Uncle tosses out a deliberately vague question to help you recap the morning discussion. "What stands out from the conversation this morning?"

You take a moment to organize your thoughts as Uncle waits. "In spite of what the critics might say, suffering only makes sense if God is real, if he is good, and if he is all-powerful. He must have good reasons to allow suffering, even if we don't always understand what those are. And that's why we ultimately have to trust in the goodness of his character."

Uncle's raised eyebrows show that he is impressed, but you're not quite finished.

"We also need to understand something about the nature of man and how he differs from the animals or else we might be inclined to just put him out of his misery like an old mutt. Man's soul is what makes him a different order of creature, and his soul makes it possible for him to reflect something of God's nature."

Uncle settles back against the chair and nods slightly. "Well said. Now that we know something about the nature of man as God created him, we have to ask an obvious question: *'What went wrong?'* Something must have gone wrong in order for us to end up in a world that is full of suffering and death."

"Are you saying that everything was good when God created it?"

"Yes, and that conclusion follows from your first observation. If God is all-good and all-powerful, then everything he creates *must* be good. It would be against the nature of a good God to create something that wasn't good."

"Then there was a time without suffering?"

"Yes, a time in the past, at the beginning of creation, where there was no suffering and no death. And there will be a time in the future when this world comes to an end, and God recreates what was once perfect."

It occurs to you, perhaps for the first time, that things were not always the way we see them today. And that our present condition is not necessarily a permanent one. "Are you saying that man was made to live forever?"

"Yes. God created man to live forever. The suffering we see today—aging, disease, disability, death—were not part of the original creation. These came *after* creation when man disobeyed God's commandment and brought about what we call the **Fall of Man**."

"But if God created man *good*, why did he disobey?"

Uncle lets out a nervous chuckle. "That is a question that not even the theologians can answer. All we can say for sure is that it happened, and that God allowed it to happen."

"But you'd argue that if a good God allowed something bad to happen, he must have had a good reason for it?"

"Yes, though we may never fully understand it."

"Okay, but can we understand it at *all*?"

"Only in the general sense, and it goes something like this. God created the universe to put his power and his glory on display. He created man upright, but with the possibility of falling from his original goodness. Man disobeyed and fell into sin, which brought all mankind under the judgment of God—which includes suffering and death. But God in his mercy has made it possible to save *some*, though all the rest are lost. Those who are saved display the glory of God's *grace*, while those who are lost display the glory of God's *judgment*."

You have to take a minute to let Uncle's explanation sink in. This is heavy stuff.

While you're still thinking, he adds the following. "The idea is that the *fullness* of God's glory is put on display in this way. If man hadn't fallen from his original perfection, God wouldn't be able to display his *judgment*. If man had fallen from perfection but none were saved from judgment, then he wouldn't be able to display his *grace*."

You know this is the critical part of the

explanation. Uncle has been building up to it all day, but it's still a lot to digest at one time.

He pauses before continuing. "These are deep waters and it's more than we can unpack at one time. I don't want you to be overwhelmed at this point."

It might be too late for that.

Chapter 10

After fetching a fresh cup of coffee, Uncle sits back down in the living room. "The important thing for you to understand at this point is that God created all things good, but man brought judgment into the world by his disobedience. As a result, all men are now guilty before God. And we are all guilty to a degree that most of us cannot begin to comprehend. The Bible puts it this way: 'there is none good—*no, not one.*'"

The conversation seems to be taking an ominous turn. Uncle has just pronounced judgment on the whole human race!

You can't allow his statement to go unchallenged—and he doesn't expect you to. "You seem to be ignoring the fact that people do good all the time. People like Michelle—a woman who was busy raising a family when she found out she was dying of a brain tumor."

Uncle senses your escalating emotions. He knows he touched a nerve. "This is a hard teaching, and few are prepared to accept it." He slows his cadence. "But we cannot understand the universal experience of *suffering* if we do not first understand the universal *guilt* of man."

Your agitation hasn't waned at all. "Are you saying we all suffer because we all *deserve* it? Are you saying *Michelle* deserves to die?"

Uncle slumps forward in his chair and leans on his knees. Without looking up, he quietly replies, "Yes. That is *precisely* what I'm saying. 'The wages of sin is death.'"

Chapter 11

In the silence of the living room you can hear the rain picking up again, as if to reflect the somber tone that has fallen over the conversation. Universal guilt. Universal suffering. *Michelle deserves to die.*

Your anger is returning as you let the words sink in. Just when you were starting to gain some confidence in the goodness of God, he is suddenly taking on a sinister appearance. Uncle seems to have painted himself into a corner this time.

Before you can put words to your thoughts, Uncle speaks again. "I need you to understand that I am not speaking in a way that exults in the suffering of your neighbor and her family. I can speak the truth even when it breaks my heart. I have no doubt that when Michelle's doctor brought her the diagnosis, there was no joy in that moment for him. He doesn't want to see his patients die. But as a doctor, he must speak the truth to his patients even when the prognosis is grim."

What Uncle is saying makes sense. Only a cruel doctor would enjoy delivering bad news to a patient. Only a cruel doctor would enjoy seeing his patients suffer. But what about God? Isn't God answerable for the kind of suffering Michelle is facing? *Can't he stop it?* And if so, why *won't* he?

Uncle seems to be reading your thoughts. "It's true that God has allowed this to happen. It's true that he could have prevented it. Even now, he could stop it. He could cure Michelle. Can I explain why he doesn't? No. I can only trust that he is far wiser than I am."

"You must have some idea, or else there isn't much point to our discussion."

Uncle senses your frustration. "I can offer

some possibilities based on what I know from the Bible. But none of those may sufficiently explain what Michelle is experiencing right now."

Chapter 12

Uncle takes a long breath as he leans back in the chair and begins to redirect the conversation. “We’ve talked about the Fall of Man and the principle of universal guilt. Perhaps we should start there.”

“Back to ‘generalities’?” you reply with a bite of sarcasm.

Uncle ignores the dig. “Yes. Principles that apply across the board. Issues that relate to God’s character and man’s condition of guilt. We’ve talked about the goodness of God, but now I want to give it another name. I want to talk about his *holiness*.”

“How is that going to help us?”

“Think of it as a study in contrasts. We have to understand just how *good* God is and just how *bad* man is. God is unblemished in his moral perfection. His law reflects his character. But he requires all of his creatures to adhere to his law. He is not only perfect, but he requires perfection. That is the definition of what it means to be holy. There is no grading on a curve with God."

"That's absurd. No one is perfect."

"You are quite right on both counts. Fallen man is neither perfect, nor is he able to achieve perfection. But God demands perfection just the same."

"That sounds completely unreasonable. And you're going to tell me that because we are not absolutely perfect, we do not have God's favor?"

"An understatement, I'm afraid. Because we are not 'perfect,' we have earned only his *judgment.* And that describes the natural condition of man after the Fall. In fact, the Bible describes us as *enemies* of God. Deserving of his wrath."

"It doesn't seem fair that God won't take

our good deeds into account."

"There are two problems with that statement. First, we don't perform any deeds that meet God's standard of *goodness*—which is absolute perfection. Secondly, God determines the standard of *fairness*, and it's based on his law—which is based on his own character."

"So you're looking for an excuse by pointing out that God doesn't compromise."

"Before you're inclined to impugn God's character, let me gently remind you that you were in complete agreement a little while ago that everything God creates is good. Man was created morally perfect, but he brought judgment on himself by willful disobedience. God's standard hasn't changed, but man in his fallen condition now wants God to lower the bar. He can't do that without violating his justice. If God could change, he wouldn't be God."

"So even *one* sin is enough to deserve judgment?"

Uncle laughs out loud in spite of himself. "Yes, but there's literally no one who's only guilty of 'one' sin. In our fallen condition, we sin *all the time*. Even when we try to do good, we still sin—in no small part because we pretentiously think our works are good enough to earn some merit."

"If what you're saying is true, then no one can please God—and presumably, no one can get into heaven."

"The Bible addresses that very objection with the response, 'what is impossible with men is possible with God.' It's why our salvation must be a work of God's grace, because our human works will never be good enough."

You're still not sure you can believe that man is all that bad—especially people like Michelle.

Uncle offers a concluding thought. "Many years ago a famous theologian expressed the problem this way: 'The only thing man contributes to his salvation is the sin that makes it necessary.'"

And as if by a flash of insight you reply, "Which is why you say God is 'glorified' in our salvation."

"Yes. Because he must do it all from beginning to end, or else no one can be saved."

Chapter 13

At this point in the afternoon, a pot of fresh coffee sounds like a really good idea. Your nerves are starting to calm a bit after wrestling with some difficult theology. Uncle said it would take patience to work through your questions, so you shouldn't be surprised that it's been a roller coaster ride. He said it would be *methodical.* You're still not there yet, but maybe you're beginning to see where the discussion is leading.

As the coffee maker completes it cycle, you pour yourself a cup and offer some to Uncle, who thanks you for the fresh cup. After stirring in the cream and sugar, you both head back into the living room. The living room lights are on as clouds darken the sky, and it's hard to tell the time of day. Outside, street lamps are already glowing.

Uncle takes a sip of coffee and starts in a slow cadence. "I realize we've covered some difficult ideas. No one likes to be confronted with the guilt of sin. It's actually part of our prideful fallen nature to evaluate ourselves favorably. But it's a terrible case of self-deception that only compounds our guilt. Denying it only makes things worse."

You break into Uncle's train of thought. "Are you going to tell me that Michelle is dying of a brain tumor because of something she did? Some terrible sin we don't know about?"

Uncle remains calm. "I could say that you're asking a valid question, but it's not one we're likely to find an answer for. Certainly, there are times when people suffer from the consequences of their own sinful choices. Drugs. Alcohol. Crime. That sort of thing. But it isn't always possible to explain a *particular* affliction in terms of a *particular* sin."

You sense that Uncle has more to say.

He continues. "In the Bible, one of the most startling examples of human suffering is seen in the life of a man named Job. There is an entire book dedicated to his experience of suffering. Neither he nor his friends are able to unravel the mystery. They are asking some valid questions. But unlike the people in Job's story, the reader sees another part of the story. We are shown the conversation between Satan and God that launches Job's odyssey of suffering."

"The spiritual reality that you referred to."

"Yes. When the human side of the story doesn't make sense, there may be a spiritual side to the story that we can't see. Job didn't see it, nor did his friends. In the end, it was God who put Job on the witness stand, not the other way around. And Job knew that he could not answer God's examination."

"So he didn't get the answer to his own suffering."

"He did not. Think about it. He lost all ten of his children, most of his servants, and most of his possessions. Afterward, he was afflicted with an assortment of dreadful diseases that made him repulsive to everyone around him. And yet this was a man who had been scrupulous in his desire to live a life pleasing to God—much more than most. He's the last person you would expect to see suffer like this."

"You're saying it could happen to anybody."

"It can and it *does*. You know that from your own experience."

"Even Christians?"

Uncle laughs again. "God's people are blessed with an array of rich promises, but there are a number of promises that would give anyone second thoughts. Fractured family relationships. Physical hardship. Ridicule. Persecution. Poverty. Prison. Torture. Even death. There's a good reason why we're warned to 'count the cost' before we decide to follow Christ."

"But don't some Christians teach that you can have all the best in this life? That you can be healed of all your diseases?"

"To suppose that the Christian life is an easy life goes against both experience and scripture. There are no such promises in the Bible. There are *blessings* in this life—even in the midst of suffering—but deliverance from suffering is only a promise for the life to come."

"Then where do those ideas come from?"

"To make a long story short, it's easy to prove anything from the Bible if you're selective enough. All you have to do is take parts of several passages, rip them out of context, fill in the gaps with your own distorted theology, and there you go. It's a form of deception that Satan is quite familiar with."

"But aren't there all kinds of healing miracles in the Bible? Wasn't Jesus a miraculous healer?"

"Healing and other miracles are indeed part of the narrative. But these miracles largely serve the purpose of confirming the divine authority of those performing the miracles—Christ and his apostles, who founded the church. Miraculous signs are not intended for all ages. And then there's the obvious problem: take a look around, and everyone who was ever healed or raised from the dead is still *dead*. The miracles were all—shall we say—*temporary* in their effects."

You look across the coffee table with a puzzled expression.

"Back to Job again. The story has a happy

ending. He was healed from his bodily diseases. God restored his possessions—double, in fact. God gave him ten more children, including three daughters who are described as the most beautiful in the land. He lived another 140 years—long enough to see his great grandchildren. All tremendous blessings. But this restoration was only temporary. Job died, along with all of his family. But before he died, he was already looking forward to a day when he would be given a new body in which he could stand before God."

"A new body to live forever—like man was intended from the beginning?"

"Yes. But that eternal life is no longer possible in our fallen bodies. We all must die in order to be permanently healed of our infirmities. To be freed from our present sufferings."

“So death is a liberation from the suffering of sin.”

“Yes, but only for the redeemed.”

Chapter 14

Only for the redeemed. The words ring in your ears. Then what about the rest of humanity? You won't have a chance to ask the question before Uncle rumbles on.

"We've established one of the most important principles of universal suffering—universal *sin.* From that we can understand that all men *die* because all men *sin.* Now we can develop some additional theology around suffering. How God can use it. Or more precisely, how he *promises* to use it."

The idea that God has made promises regarding suffering is a bit unexpected. Once again you find yourself recalling that Uncle asked for patience when the conversation started this morning.

"You may not like what I have to say next, but it has important ramifications. We have to preserve the integrity and the power and the purposes of God. And that means we have to acknowledge that God not only *allows* suffering in the passive sense, but in fact he *ordains* it. In other words, he *wills* it."

"You're saying he *wants* it to happen? Is that really what you mean?" There is a bit of alarm in your voice. This doesn't strike you as a good way to 'preserve' the integrity of God. He's starting to sound like an ogre again.

"I know it's hard to get a handle on. It seems to suggest that God is sadistic—that he wants to hurt people. Maybe that he enjoys seeing people suffer. But we have to be careful here. Remember that if God is God, he is in complete control of the universe. Nothing happens apart from his will. By allowing the Fall of Man, and by allowing the suffering that follows, he is working out his plan of redemption."

You remain skeptical. "I'm not sure I follow."

"Let me put it this way: A good God allows suffering because he can always bring good out of it. Or to paraphrase Joseph the son of Jacob, 'whatever man intends for evil, God intends for good.' God does this sort of thing all the time. He has to, given the fallen condition of mankind. Joseph's brothers hated him and intended to kill him, but then they sold him into slavery to make a quick buck off of his demise. God ordained this treachery in order to send Joseph to Egypt where he would be able to save his family from a terrible famine. It's a remarkable illustration of how God allows evil in order to do good."

"So you're saying that if Michelle is dying from a brain tumor, even though it's tragic on a human level, that God can bring good from it?"

"Not only that he *can*, but that he *will*.

Which brings us back to the question of how suffering can be good. It's a paradox that the atheist can never unravel. But for the Christian, there is always meaning and purpose in suffering."

Uncle still has a lot of work to do if he's going to change your mind about that.

Chapter 15

After a moment to reflect, you now have a different thought rattling around in your head. Uncle skated by it but you want to know more. "You said that God brings good out of evil because he *has* to."

Uncle takes the cue even though you didn't ask a question. "Yes. Remember how we established that the universal condition of man is sinful. The verdict is severe. The Bible says, for example, that 'the heart is deceitful above all else and desperately sick' and '*all* the thoughts of man's heart are only evil *continually'* and that '*all* have sinned and fallen short of the glory of God.' Those are just a few examples of the verdict against fallen man. If it's true that we are—to coin an expression—'all sin all the time,' then what exactly does God have to work with in the way of raw materials?"

You see Uncle's point. "God has to bring good out of evil because he doesn't have anything good to start with."

"He literally doesn't have anything else to work with."

Suddenly you're thunderstruck by the character of a God who can bring good out of evil and who chooses to do so rather than just scrapping the whole affair. The words tumble out of your mouth. "Instead of bringing good out of evil, God could just start over."

"Yes. God could destroy the world and condemn the lost. Wipe the slate clean. It would be, as we said, an expression of his glory in judgment. And he's come close to doing that on more than one occasion. But by preserving the fallen creation and bringing good out it—and by saving some of the lost—he demonstrates the glory of his kindness and grace."

You're starting to see this God of the Bible in a whole new way.

Chapter 16

Uncle charges ahead. “If we want to understand the matter of suffering in the present life, we need to think about the suffering that awaits for those who remain under God’s judgment.”

“I suppose you’re referring to hell.”

“Yes. It is the place where all the lost are sent to pay for their particular sins. It is the place where God metes out his righteous judgment on all those who live in rebellion to him and who stubbornly refuse to repent and receive the gospel of his free grace.”

Uncle has said a mouthful, but he apparently intends to defuse your natural resistance to the idea of hell as something cruel and unusual.

He goes on. “Remember we talked about God’s holiness. That his character is moral perfection, and he demands moral perfection. And because he is holy, he is also *just*—meaning that his holy character requires giving to every man precisely what he deserves. Nothing more or less."

"But you've already said that man can do nothing to earn favor with God."

"Not in his fallen condition. All he can do is add to his own guilt—no matter how hard he tries."

"So justice means getting what he deserves."

"That's the definition of justice. And that means punishment for sin—in hell. And because in his sinful nature the fallen man never repents, he only adds to his guilt even as he's being punished for sin. Which is one of the reasons why hell is forever."

"The thought of hell is terrifying."

"As it should be. It's one of the reasons we're told to fear God—because he has the power to destroy both body and soul in hell. But sinful men are neither sensible of their guilt nor fearful of a just judge. They are unaware of the fact that God is storing up his wrath for the day of their judgment. Think of it like water building up behind a huge dam, waiting to burst out in a catastrophic deluge."

"If hell is as bad as you make it sound, it has to be much worse than anything we experience in this life."

"Correct. Which brings me to the first key idea: Suffering in *this* life ought to make us sensible to the danger of suffering in the *next*. It ought to make us afraid of hell."

"Because hell will be worse."

"The suffering of the lost in hell is unimaginably worse than any suffering that takes place in this life. Man may complain bitterly about the pains of this life while having no idea of the pain that awaits after death."

“So in a sense, this life spares him from the next.”

“Only for a while. As the Bible says, God is patient toward us so that we have time to repent. We are without excuses. But it also says that God has appointed a day on which all men will be judged by Jesus Christ according to their deeds.”

“But some who are afflicted in this life will be saved?”

“Yes. God often brings suffering into the life of the unbeliever in order to lead him to salvation. To shatter his confidence in himself so that he turns to God.”

“And that is good.”

“Very good indeed.”

Chapter 17

Before Uncle says any more, you offer a quick recap. “I think I see how suffering can bring someone who’s lost to salvation. But the next question is why someone who’s already saved should suffer. You would say they are going to heaven. So what’s the point of suffering? What do they have to gain?”

Uncle nods slightly. He sees how much you’ve learned already—and that you’re now getting a step ahead of the conversation.

“Let’s start by thinking about the immediate effect of suffering in the life of a believer. The Bible promises that God will bring good out of it. Suffering has the effect of loosening our attachment on the present life and pointing us toward the life to come. In short, suffering draws us closer to God.”

"And that's good because we get too attached to things of this life?"

"Yes. We all have the tendency to place too much value on the things that will soon pass away. And we place too much confidence in our own strength. Suffering pulls us away from temporary things, including self-confidence."

"You said a while ago that we have to die in order to put an end to suffering."

"For the believer, death becomes the passageway not only to heaven, but to that future day when the sinful body is replaced with a new body that lives forever. This is the hope of the resurrection."

"That's what Job was looking forward to?"

"Yes, because the body we occupy now will only continue to decay as we approach the end of life. The Bible says that our mortal flesh is 'wasting away'—which refers to old age, infirmity, disease, and eventually death.

Any healing we experience in this life—no matter how miraculous—is only temporary. This mortal body *must* return to the dust so that it can be remade in the time to come."

"Is it ever the case that suffering for the Christian is a result of sin?"

"Quite often, in fact. God promises to bring discipline on those he loves, and we know discipline involves different kinds of suffering. Some of it is bodily and some of it is spiritual—meaning the pain of a wounded conscience. And in many cases, suffering is the natural result of our choices. Sin still has consequences. God saves us so that we can be freed *from* sin, which means we are freed *for* obedience to his law. The Bible calls it *sanctification*—being set apart. It means that we are becoming more like Christ. But it is a lifelong process that isn't completed until death."

"Moral perfection is the goal?"

"Always. Perfection is the goal of our salvation. God can never compromise in regard to his law. Suffering is one of the ways we grow. It isn't 'torture' because it is done in love—as the love of a father to his children."

"Could we say that God uses suffering as a teacher?"

"Absolutely. It is a guide that steers us along the right path and corrects us when we begin to stray."

"Like a bad grade in school or a bad review at work."

"Yes. But even Christians can be quite stubborn, so it often takes considerable discomfort to get our attention. Sometimes it even takes a tragedy."

"But the momentary pain of *correction* is what steers us away from the ultimate pain of *destruction.*"

"That's a good way to put it. But it isn't the case for everyone."

Chapter 18

Uncle has just opened another can of worms. He forges ahead. “There’s another important purpose for suffering. It separates true believers from false ones—because the Bible makes it clear that not everyone who *claims* to be a Christian is *actually* a Christian.”

“And how does suffering figure into that difference?”

“As we’ve seen, one of the promises God makes to the Christian is that he can expect to suffer for his faith. You might say there is always a test of faith. The Bible explains that true faith is too precious *not* to test. In fact, it likens our faith to gold that is tested and refined by fire. Purified and perfected, as it were. And fire is merely a metaphor for suffering.”

"You've already described how suffering is used for the benefit of the believer."

"Correct. Now consider what happens when someone *claiming* to be a Christian is tested. Placed into the 'fiery trial.' What's going to happen?"

"If he's expecting God to make his life easy, he may start to turn against God when the going gets tough."

"Not only that, but he'll probably abandon the faith. He'll walk away from the church."

"And that's *good*?"

"In the short term, it's good for the church when false believers leave. It's also good—in a certain sense—for the one who leaves, because it exposes his false profession. He cannot continue to deceive himself in regard to his faith. He has to confront his own unbelief. And that may be what leads him to true faith later on."

"So, many will stay in church as long as

it's comfortable. As long as it meets their expectations."

"In fact, that's how a great many people end up in the church in the first place. The church often compromises in regard to doctrine, and places more emphasis on *attracting* people than on *instructing* them. Many end up deceived. Perhaps *most.*"

"And that makes for a weaker church."

"A strong church is not defined in terms of its size or its popularity or its budget, but in terms of its *faithfulness.* These days it isn't hard to find big churches that have basically no influence. They are entertainment centers. They don't have the truth, and there is never any real power apart from the truth."

"What happens if the culture starts to turn against the church?"

"That's the definition of persecution. And when it comes, we can expect to see a great 'falling away.' Many will leave the church at that point."

"But only because they weren't true believers in the first place."

"True believers will always persevere. They *never* abandon the church."

"True believers like Job?"

"Job struggled enormously through his trials, but in the end, he passed the test."

Chapter 19

Since you were already anticipating another long day of discussion, you made a point to pick up a pasta casserole for dinner. It's been in the oven for the last hour or so, filling the house with the delightful aroma of cheese and Italian spices. The timer is hardly necessary to signal the dinner hour. You and Uncle take your places at the kitchen table and start digging into the bubbly dish. A loaf of buttery garlic bread completes the spread. The hot meal is a fitting contrast to the damp chill on a rainy day like this.

Dinner is attended by more small talk as you tell Uncle about some of the things you're learning at work—and some of the obstacles you're running into. It's becoming more comfortable after the first few months, and much of the mystery and anxiety of being in a new environment is fading. There are new rules to learn, and new ways to measure your progress. You're getting used to working as part of a team, which is a stark contrast to the individual recognition you were accustomed to as a college student. But you're also starting to see the roadblocks. It's a reminder that school didn't prepare you all that well for the workplace, except that you still rely on your ability to learn and apply new knowledge. You can tell that Uncle enjoys talking about the workplace culture, which might one day make for an interesting discussion in its own right. He peppers you with questions until it's time to clear the table and get back to the business at hand.

Chapter 20

By the time you finish dinner and return to the living room, it has been dark for a while. The rain has now stopped along with the rumbles of thunder. The storm has apparently moved on.

Your conversation today has taken a number of unexpected turns and seems to be winding down. The hardest part by far was confronting the universal state of man under the judgment of sin. You're not yet used to thinking in terms of God requiring moral perfection from his creatures. It seems that you have always taken your *imperfection* for granted and wrongly assumed that God would grade your performance on a curve—much as you're inclined to grade yourself. Partial credit for effort, and that sort of thing.

Uncle abruptly returns to the subject of

suffering. "We've looked at the ways in which suffering works in the lives of those who are suffering, so now let's consider how suffering affects others in the immediate vicinity. What should our response be when we see someone else suffering?"

The answer seems obvious. "Our response is to provide care and encouragement to the one who's suffering."

"Let's call it *compassion.* And it can take many forms. Are you familiar with the parable of the Good Samaritan?"

"Isn't it about helping a guy who's been hurt?"

"Yes. A man fell among thieves, was stripped naked and beaten to within an inch of his life, and dumped alongside the road. His Jewish brethren—clergymen, actually—passed by without stopping to help, but a Samaritan had compassion on him and bound up his wounds."

“The Samaritan was willing to get involved.”

“Let’s be even more specific. The Samaritan was willing to enter into the suffering of the wounded Jew. He wasn’t just offering aid. It was personal, even though the Jew was a stranger—and an enemy.”

“But those who passed by were indifferent. Callous.”

“So how does the suffering of others reveal something about the disposition of our own hearts?”

“I suppose it’s sort of a test to see whether we care enough to show compassion toward others.”

“And do you get the sense from the parable that the Samaritan was ‘burdened’ by turning aside to help a wounded Jew?”

“Hardly. He seems to see it as a duty, or maybe even a privilege.”

“The Samaritan was willing to sacrifice

his own time and resources to help someone in need. Meanwhile, the Jews who passed by couldn't even be troubled to help one of their own countrymen."

"They failed the test."

Chapter 21

"God summarizes his law in two great commandments: to love God with all our heart, mind, soul, and strength, and to love our neighbor as ourselves. Jesus spoke the parable of the Good Samaritan in answer to the question, 'Who is my neighbor?' It was a painful lesson for the Jews because they hated the Samaritans and wanted nothing to do with them. The parable exposed the hardness of their hearts—their hypocrisy. It showed that they did not grasp what it meant to love one's neighbor. They considered themselves righteous but couldn't even be moved to have compassion on one of their own brethren who was violently assaulted and left for dead. Someone who certainly didn't ask for the suffering that came upon him."

"So the suffering of others is an opportunity to show compassion—true love—toward the one who is suffering."

"And how does that shed new light on Michelle's condition?"

"Well, I suppose we could look at her illness as an opportunity for her friends and family to care for her, and for them to care for her family after she dies."

"And?"

Ouch. You have to swallow hard. "And an opportunity for her neighbors to show compassion, as well."

"Perhaps that is the test that God has placed in front of *you* right now. You can either pass by—which is the easy way out—or you can come alongside and offer to help."

"Tragedy can bring us closer together as friends and neighbors . . . if we allow it to. God can use the suffering of another for *our* good, as well."

It’s all starting to make sense.

Chapter 22

"I stated at the outset that we probably wouldn't answer all of your questions today. We're trying to understand some intensely personal matters of faith and life that are grounded in deep theological concepts. But we've covered a lot of important ground."

"This has been a big help to me." You're relieved and overwhelmed at the same time.

Uncle continues. "Suffering is a topic that hits close to home for all of us, sooner or later. Michelle's diagnosis has forced you to confront some hard questions at a stage in life when most people your age are little concerned about suffering and death. For young people, it seems too far off to be concerned about it. Friends, family, and career are more likely to dominate your priorities."

"I can't help thinking that if something

tragic could happen to Michelle. . . ." You're afraid to finish the thought.

"Of course. It could happen to *you*. That's a hard truth to face, but it's part of the lesson. In reality, we are *all* living under a terminal diagnosis. Just like Michelle. It's only a matter of time."

"I've been taking my life for granted—believing that I will live to a ripe old age where I'll get to see and do all the normal things of life."

"And you probably will. But we still have to be reminded that it's God who numbers our days from beginning to end. For *his* purposes. For *his* glory. Our lives are a gift from him that we shouldn't take for granted. And even those who are blessed with length of days will discover that the time goes by quickly. As Jacob, the patriarch of Israel, said to the king of Egypt, 'the days of my life have been few and full of evil.' He was 130 years old when he said that!"

Chapter 23

The empty house is silent as you sit in the living room reflecting on the day's conversation. Uncle left an hour ago and is probably home by now. He's right that you still have questions. You're still struggling to understand why there is so much suffering in the world and how God uses it for good. How he displays his mercy in sustaining a world full of pain and how he uses fallen people to show compassion to each other. How he is patient in offering grace and mercy to those who are rebels deserving judgment.

Michelle's diagnosis is no less tragic than when you started the conversation this morning, but you're already thinking about how you can reach out to this family in their time of trial. The only question is how you'll muster the courage to show compassion—to 'enter into their suffering,' as Uncle explained it. And if you do, that *you* might never be the same.

Review Questions

You may find the following questions helpful to review key ideas in the book and/or use this book for group study and discussion.

1. How does the reality of suffering tempt us to question the goodness of God?
2. When have you been most severely confronted with the reality of suffering?
3. Why is it so tempting to blame God for suffering?
4. Why does it require more than human experience in order to understand the nature of suffering?
5. How does the position of the atheist fail to account for the reality of suffering?
6. How does the atheist try to use the reality

of suffering to impugn God's character?

7. Explain the *imago Dei.* How is man unique in creation? In what ways does he reflect the nature of his Creator?
8. Why does science fail to recognize the unique attributes of man?
9. How does the Fall of Man explain the presence of suffering and death?
10. How does the universal guilt of man account for the universal experience of suffering?
11. Why must truth take precedence over feelings?
12. How does God's goodness make it impossible for him to lower his standard?
13. How does Job's experience of suffering illustrate how there's often "more than meets the eye"?
14. What is the explanation for why a good God would ordain suffering?
15. Why is it necessary—in a fallen world—

for God to bring good out of evil?

16. How should the experience of suffering in this life serve as a warning about suffering in the next life?
17. How does God use suffering as a means to sanctify the believer?
18. What purposes are served by God testing someone's faith "by fire"?
19. Why is it that church growth is not enough by itself to know that people are being saved?
20. What does the parable of the Good Samaritan teach us about showing compassion to the one who is afflicted?
21. Which of your neighbors are in need of your help? What can you do to show compassion?
22. How has this book helped you think about your own life? How might it change your priorities?

Glossary

contradiction—opposing ideas that are in conflict in such a way that they cannot both be correct.

Darwinism—the belief that new species are formed by descent when modifications that prove favorable in the struggle for survival are passed from one generation to the next.

ethics—the branch of philosophy that considers the question of right and wrong.

Fall of Man—the event following creation when Adam and Eve, though created perfect, brought ruin upon themselves and the world by their disobedience to God's command.

imago Dei—literally, "the image of God;" the communicable traits of God that were given to man at creation, including an immortal soul. The *imago Dei* sets man apart from all the rest of creation and it establishes the theological basis for the sanctity of human life.

metaphysics (metaphysical)—the branch of philosophy that addresses nonmaterial reality.

paradox— an apparent conflict of ideas that is resolved with additional information.

premises—statements that serve as the basis for an argument.

syllogism—a form of argument where premises are used to draw a logical conclusion.

teleology—the branch of philosophy that addresses meaning or purpose.

worldview—the beliefs that one holds regarding the nature of reality; philosophy.

Acknowledgements

Many thanks to my readers and reviewers for your helpful suggestions. Your feedback is always appreciated.

About the Author

J.R. Dickens completed a Ph.D. in mechanical engineering and enjoys writing and speaking on topics like philosophy, ethics, and Christian apologetics. He can be reached by email at jrdickens90@gmail.com.

J.R.'s books are available on Amazon.